The
GREATEST
TREASURE

by Anne Lacourrege
illustrated by Joshua Wichterich

To my dad, Harry, who was always a kid at heart looking for treasure.

To my kids, Michael and Patrick, who helped me to see the world anew.

And to my husband, Chuck, who always believes in me.

Once upon a time, there was a little girl named Lily. She was an only child who lived in a lovely, old house built in the 1800's. The house looked like an old ship. This was no coincidence since it was built by a sea captain, Harry the Pirate.

The house was two stories high and subdivided into four apartments. The apartments went straight through like your typical New Orleans shot-gun house. Lily and her parents lived upstairs in one apartment. The two downstairs apartments were rented out to folks. The house belonged to Lily's grandmother.

The upstairs apartments could open into one another through two possible doorways. One doorway connected the two kitchens and always remained open.

The other doorway was never opened. It seemed to connect one apartment's bedroom with the other apartment's dining room. This doorway always seemed mysterious to Lily. It was her bedroom that had the closed doorway.

Lily was always curious as to the closed doorway.
She often asked for someone to open it.
Her parents and grandmother always said the
the same thing, "No one has the key."

Lily sometimes had dreams about what was behind the doorway. One night she thought she heard someone asking her to open the door. It was a man's voice. When Lily woke up, there was no one there. She went to sleep again and slept through the rest of the night.

The next day Lily was playing in the basement. There was a very old desk there that no one had touched in years. She was playing wall ball. The ball flew past her and accidentally hit the desk leg. Suddenly out of the bottom of the desk, there fell a silver key. It was long and looked very old. Lily picked it up and looked at the key. It looked like such a treasure. She placed the key in her pocket and went back to playing ball.

Dusk came and Lily went upstairs. It was supper time. Lily told her parents and grandmother about the key. No one could imagine who put the key under the desk or what it opened.

That night, Lily's mom was putting Lily to bed. Once again, Lily looked at her new treasure. She held on to it as her mother read a bedtime story. As Lily drifted off to sleep, the key fell to her side. Her mom moved the key to the night stand. As the night wore on, Lily again heard a voice calling her to open the door. Again, she said she didn't have the key. The voice responded that she did.

Lily realized the key she found was the key to the
doorway. She spotted the key on the night stand.
As she moved closer to the door, she began to
feel a little scared. She was so curious about the
doorway for so long that she wanted to open the
the door, but who was calling to her and what
would she find? The voice reassured her that it
was okay. The voice sounded very kind.

Lily placed the key in the doorway lock. She turned
the key and she heard a click. This is the moment
she had waited for so long. She was still afraid,
but she was determined to find out what was
behind this door.

Lily could not believe her eyes. There was a hidden room that was triangular in shape nestled between the two apartments. It was well lit and cheery. It was filled with furniture, coloring books and colors, playing cards, checker boards and checkers, and all kinds of toys. There was beautiful art work on the walls and an artist's tripod and paints. There was also a large chest that was black with gold trim. As Lily looked around in awe, a little man appeared. As he spoke, Lily recognized the voice as the one she had been hearing the past several nights. The man introduced himself as Captain Harry. He spoke very kindly to Lily.

Captain Harry thanked her for opening the door. He had been trapped within this hidden room. He was the one who had built this house for his lovely wife and daughter.

This room was especially built as a hide out for them in the event anyone would break into the house. It was set up with items to keep them amused and cared for. It was built in what was a very isolated location at the time along the banks of the Mississippi River. Back then, pirates would some times sail along the river and try to cause trouble for folks who lived along its river banks. Captain Harry loved his family and was very protective of them. Unfortunately as much as we love our dear ones, bad things sometimes happen. His wife and daughter had gone to the French Market to shop. While they were out, the captain noticed the weather began to change quickly. He became very concerned.

He was looking out for their return. As he stood on the porch,
he could see them coming home. Suddenly the rain came down
and the levee broke, an avalanche of water came rushing down
on his family.

He ran to help them, but he was too late. Neither his wife or daughter could swim; they floated down the river never to be heard from again. The captain returned home. He missed his family and grieved heavily. He closed himself up in his room and had eventually spent what seemed to be an eternity there. Next thing, he heard Lily's family moving into his house. He felt the presence once again of the love of family...Lily's family. This had softened his heart again, and he once again longed for his own family. He finally forgave himself for his family's misfortune. This in return allowed his spirit to be free. He could finally leave behind his heavy chain that was made of sorrow, bitterness and loneliness. He realized that life is a journey and not just something that randomly happens. With the doorway locked, he could not join his family. He wanted to share this special hideaway spot and his story with Lily and her family. He hoped they would understand why it took so long for him to learn.

Captain Harry asked Lily to open the black and gold
chest. When she did, there were Spanish
doubloons, pearls, rubies and other treasures. Lily
was so excited and so touched by the captain's
kindness. Lily ran to tell her family. As Lily's
family came into the room, they were in awe just
like Lily had been. However, the captain was
gone. Lily told her family what had happened.
Her family was surprised, but was very doubtful
about there being a Captain Harry.

Suddenly, there was a very bright light. In front of them all stood a gentleman, a lady and a young girl. The gentleman smiled and told Lily thank you. They waved farewell and faded into the heavens. Lily's family was overjoyed.

From one family to another, they realized that the greatest treasure is love. A family's love for one another can never be ignored or replaced. It truly is the greatest treasure of all.

Made in the USA
Columbia, SC
20 February 2024